Down the Drain

Stories linking with the History
National Curriculum Key Stage 2

First published in 1999 by Franklin Watts
96 Leonard Street, London EC2A 4XD

Editor: Sarah Snashall
Designer: Jason Anscomb
Consultant: Dr Anne Millard, BA Hons, Dip Ed, PhD

A CIP catalogue record for this book
is available from the British Library.

ISBN   0 7496 3357 3 (hbk)
          0 7496 3550 9 (pbk)

Dewey Classification 941.081

Printed in Great Britain

Down the Drain

by
Jon Blake

Illustrations by Greg Gormley

W

FRANKLIN WATTS
NEW YORK • LONDON • SYDNEY

1
The map

I pulled the chain for the fifth time. It was the most amazing thing I'd ever seen. A great gush of water filled the toilet bowl, then it all went down like a whirlpool. "Stanley!" came a shout. "Is that you in there again?"

It was Grandma. She was worried about the amount of time I was spending in the privy. But since they'd put this new W.C. in, it was the most exciting place in the house. Well, just outside the house, to be precise.

W.C. It stood for water closet. Not many people had them yet. Most still had the old privy midden, which was just a hole over a box, or an ash pail, which got collected once a week. Some just used the nearest alley or chucked their doings out of the window.

Some W.C.s, like ours, were connected

to the drains. But most waste still went into a stinking cesspit. If you were lucky, this was outside the house. If you were unlucky, it was underneath the floor. If you were really unlucky and the floorboards were dodgy, you could end up swimming in it. That's what happened to Charlie Piggott round the corner. He's not with us anymore.

You might think our house smelled great with a W.C. You'd be wrong. There was this one odour which never went away – the odour that came from Dad.

None of us could understand it. I

mean, the whole of London stank, and most of the people in it, but none of us were in the same league as Dad. He gave off an odour like rotting cabbage, dead bodies and dog dung, all rolled into one. Even our pig kept its distance from him.
There must be a reason for it, I kept telling myself. But Dad had a perfectly clean job. He worked indoors, as a shipping clerk. He had to walk past the slaughterhouse to get to work, but so did lots of people, and they didn't smell like Dad.

Anyway, that's enough about filth and

bad smells. On with the story.

Just as I was about to flush the toilet bowl one last time, I noticed a corner of paper sticking out from behind the water tank. Hello, I thought. This looks interesting.

I stood on the rim of the toilet bowl and eased the piece of paper out into the light. It was quite large and carefully folded. I sat down, unfolded it, and studied the contents. What it was I couldn't say. It looked like some kind of map, but there were no street names on it, just loads of lines crossing each other, some thin, some fat.

Suddenly there was a hammering at the door. Grandma. There was no time to replace the paper, so I stuffed it into my trousers and took it away with me.

2

Dad's map

It soon became obvious that Dad had lost
something. He poked around the kitchen
range and explored the chairs. He visited
the privy at least six times. It was no
surprise when he arrived at the door of the
room which I shared with my three brothers.

"Has anyone taken anything which is not theirs?" he asked.

Dad could only mean the strange sheet of paper.

"What kind of thing, Dad?" I asked, innocently.

"Just ... a thing," replied Dad.

"Is this thing wooden? Metal? Paper?"

"Never mind," said Dad, who was getting more and more uncomfortable.

"If you can't tell me what it is," I replied, "how do I know if I've taken it?"

"All right," said Dad, gruffly. "It's a map."

So it was a map!

"A map of what?" I asked, even more innocently.

"A map," grunted Dad, "of London's sewers."

So that was what it was! But whatever did Dad want with a map of the sewers?

"Is this it?" I asked, flourishing the folded paper.

"Where did you get that?" snapped

Dad. He marched towards me, in a cloudy odour of cat-sick and rotten fish.

As I went to cover my nose, he snatched the map away.

"It was in the W.C., Dad," I replied. "I just found it on the ground. Dad, why have you got a map of the sewers?"

I could see Dad was struggling for an excuse, but none came to him. "We'd better have a talk," he said.

3

Dad's secret

Dad puffed hard on his old pipe. He
obviously had a weight on his mind.

"Son," he said, "I've been living a lie
for the past twenty years."

"How do you mean, Dad?"

"Your grandfather – your mum's father

– was a very strict man. He wouldn't allow his daughter to marry a man without prospects. So I made up this story about being a shipping clerk."

"You're not a clerk? Then … what are you?"

Dad coughed awkwardly. "A sewer inspector," he replied.

"So that explains the smell!" I blurted.

Dad frowned. "What smell?" he asked.

"Oh – nothing," I replied.

I tried to make sense of it all. "A sewer

inspector," I repeated. "But isn't that a good job?"

"It is a very fine and important job," replied Dad. "But your grandfather would never have seen that. As soon as he knew I spent my days knee-deep in other people's filth, I would have been out on my ear. So you must swear never to tell your mother this terrible secret."

"I swear."

Dad sighed deeply while my imagination worked overtime. I tried to picture the maze of tunnels on Dad's map, a whole city under the city.

"What's it like down there?" I asked, eagerly.

"In some places it's so cramped I'm on my hands and knees," said Dad. "But the new tunnels, they're a miracle. Huge underground caverns, stretching for miles. You see, with so many people, and all these W.C.s, the river was becoming like a huge cesspit. They had to build these new tunnels to take the waste away, further down-river, or off to the sewage works."

I had never heard Dad talk with such knowledge. My interest was growing by the second.

"Dad," I said, "will you take me down with you?"

At this, Dad's face grew stern. "Never!" he replied.

"Why not?"

"The sewer," replied Dad, "is a deeply dangerous place. A place of disease. A place of rats as big as your head. And a place of deadly gases, which can explode without warning and tear you to shreds."

With that, Dad knocked out his pipe and left the room. I knew well enough that when Dad said 'No', he meant 'No'. But I was gripped by a strange and powerful obsession, dragging me under ground like a magnet. I decided to visit my pal Bertie, to beg his oil-lamp off him, and to invite him on the adventure of a lifetime.

4
The King of the Toshers

It was collection day down Bertie's street.
There was a reeking pail outside
everybody's front door, except outside
Bertie's house. Bertie's aunty was worried
someone would nick her pail, so she just
emptied the contents on the pavement and

took it back inside.

Not everyone can have a W.C. like ours.

I rapped on the window and Bertie appeared, bleary-eyed. He'd been working all morning at the fish market, which added a few more smells to the general perfume of the street.

"Bertie," I said, "I've got an idea which will knock you out."

I told Bertie all about the map, and the stuff I'd found out about the sewers,

but I left out Dad's great secret because
Bertie had the biggest mouth in Britain.

Bertie listened
carefully but, to
my surprise, he
shook his head.

"No way I'm
going down
there," he said.

"You're not
afraid of rats,
are you?"

"Nope."

"Diseases?"

"Nope."

"Dangerous gases?"

"'Course not!"

"Then what are you afraid of?" I asked.

Bertie lowered his voice to a whisper.
"Haven't you heard," he hissed, "of the

King of the Toshers?"

"No?"

Bertie looked both ways, as if this king could be listening right now.

"Not so long ago," he whispered, "the sewers were full of toshers. A strange race of underground men, in long greasy coats with huge pockets. They crept about with the rats, searching for coins and jewels."

"There are coins in the sewers?" I blurted.

Bertie hushed me. "The sewers are full of them," he said. "Everything that gets washed down a drain ends up there."

Now that was something to add to my picture of life underground! Treasure!

"So what happened to these toshers?" I asked.

"Some say they all drowned," replied Bertie. "Some say they all died of disease, or they just couldn't get into the sewers, because big gates were built to stop them. But I think ..." Bertie drew me closer, "… he killed them all."

"The King of the Toshers?"

"Killed them and ate them."

"No!" I gasped.

Bertie nodded. His face was deadly serious.

"So who is this King of the Toshers?" I asked.

"No one knows," said Bertie. "Some say he's the Devil himself. Jessie Smith swore she saw him rise up out of a drain cover, seize a cow on its way to market, then slip back down again like smoke. Seven foot tall he was, with a hat tipped over his eyes, and a face covered in warts, and where his feet should be … just hooves. The hooves of a goat."

"Doesn't scare me," I said.

"Then why have your lips gone white?" sneered Bertie.

I put a hand to my mouth, and Bertie gave a long, slow snigger.

"Are we going down then?" I asked.

"All right," said Bertie.

5
Down the drain

It was a foul day, the day we chose to go under ground. The rain poured, the cesspits were overflowing, the factories belched sulphur, and blood from the slaughterhouse ran down the street and into the storm drains. London was drowning in its own filth.

We'd made some preparations. Bertie had his oil-lantern and both of us carried a good stout lump of wood, to brain the rats ... or anything else we might come across.

As for where to go down ... where better than the place Jessie Smith swore she saw the King of the Toshers?

We made our way through the warren
of streets and alleys, past back-to-back
houses, packed so tightly together there
was hardly room for the privies. When we
reached the famous manhole cover, Bertie
got to work lifting it, while I looked out
for crushers, which was what we called
the police.

It didn't take too long to get the cover

off. We peered into the hole, where metal rungs led down into the darkness below. I set off down, carrying the lantern, while Bertie lowered the cover behind us. It settled with a massive CLANK which echoed for miles below ground.

"Like closing the lid of your own coffin," said Bertie.

"Shut up!" I hissed.

There was no way of knowing how far we were going down. The rungs kept on coming, and a damp, stale smell rose around us. It seemed cold, far colder than above ground.

At last my feet made a landing. I held up the lantern, to see an egg-shaped tunnel of crumbling bricks, no taller than I was. The ground was flat, and a chilly stream washed around my knees. I seemed to be standing on some kind of silt. At least, I hoped it was silt.

"What can you see, Stanley?" asked Bertie.

"It's all misty," I said. "I can only see a few feet."

"Just walk," urged Bertie.

"Shouldn't we leave a trail?" I suggested. "So we can find our way back?"

"We'll remember," said Bertie.

I was far from convinced. But I was
determined not to look chicken, and so
was Bertie, so we just pressed on. We
walked for what seemed half a mile, and
nothing seemed to change.

"Why did we come this way?" I
complained.

Bertie gave a little
snivelly laugh. "How
do you know I'm not
working for the
King?" he said.

"Give over."

"Maybe he pays
me to bring him
his dinner."

Bertie laughed again, a real nasty, cruel
laugh. I swung round with the lantern,
intent on shutting him up. At that second,
the light glinted on something in the stream.

"It's … a penny! " I cried.

I bent down and snatched up the prize. A big, whole, heavy penny! I showed it to Bertie and we both did a splashy war

dance of delight.

"I *told* you there was treasure down here!" said Bertie.

We marched on with new energy. Up ahead there was a junction with another tunnel.

To our amazement, we came out into a space the size of a church, with arches, pillars, and tunnels leading out in all directions. Here the sewage became a wide, shallow river. The state of the bricks told us this was one of the new monster sewers.

"Wow!" I said, gazing around. "It really is like a city under ground."

"This is where the *real* treasure will be," said Bertie.

We made our way eagerly down this huge underground highway, with the rush of water in our ears and every smell of

London up our noses. Bertie found a flatch (that's a halfpenny), I found a farthing, and everything seemed just too good to be true.

Far too good to be true.

Then we met our first rat.

Neither of us saw it coming. It just scuttled past without warning, a great, shaggy, humped-back thing with a thick snake of a tail. I'd seen rats, but none as evil-looking as this one. Suddenly the whole sewer seemed filled with that evil. All its poisons and dangers swelled up in my mind – the fatal diseases and the fire-damp gas, hanging in the shadows above us, waiting to take us away.

"Let's go back now," I said. "We've got what we came for."

"We've only just started!" snorted Bertie.

"I've got a bad feeling about this tunnel," I said.

"Oh, poor little babby!" sneered Bertie.

"Listen!" I pleaded. "That rat ... was an omen!"

"Well," said Bertie, slamming his wooden club into his hand, "if there are any more, we'll be ready for them."

We pressed on, towards God-knows-what.

★★★

How I wished I had Dad's map with me.
We seemed to be crossing half of London,

 and every
time a little
sewer joined
us, the main
sewer seemed
to get bigger,
till it was
twice our
height. Bertie
was still
finding bits
and pieces in
the muck, but none were worth much, and
my unease was growing.

And then something very strange
occurred.

Bertie's lantern, which had been
casting a dim, bleary light, suddenly

seemed to grow brighter.

For a moment I thought it had something to do with the sewer gases. Then, in one heart-stopping moment, I discovered the true reason.

Ahead of us, there was another light.

Suddenly, horribly, the massive shadow of a man loomed to fill the tunnel.

"Get back!" I hissed to Bertie, pushing him flat against the sewer wall.

Hardly daring to breathe, I glanced up the tunnel. There ahead, picking his way through the gloom, was a tall, sinister figure in a long, greasy coat, its massive pockets bulging with dead rats and sovereigns.

Our worst nightmare was about to come true.

6
Run!

"Put out the light!" I hissed.

"How can I?" rasped Bertie. "We can't find our way back in the dark!"

Though we talked in the lowest of tones, every little sound we made seemed to echo like thunder. The King of the Toshers looked

up, like a rat catching a scent

Slowly, in his big, creaking boots, he crept towards us.

Half of me wanted to run, but my legs just wouldn't move. I could hear Bertie's breath, great shivering wheezes, in my ear. He wasn't sounding so brave now.

The King of the Toshers lifted his lantern and peered. Suddenly his head

craned forward and a sharp grunt escaped
his mouth. He'd seen us!

"Run, Bertie!"

We bolted like frightened rabbits, back
down the tunnel, filth splattering up our
legs. Behind us, like fate itself, came the
thunderous boots of the foul King. He was
older than us, but he knew his way round
these tunnels. Besides, Bertie was getting

short of breath. He had
nearly died of
bronchitis when
he was small and
he'd never really
recovered.

We got out of the
main sewer, back into
the smaller side tunnel.
Bertie stopped, doubled
up, and fought for
breath.

"Is he ... still coming?"
he gasped.

I listened out. Yes, he was still coming,
and not far behind.

"Maybe we could ... fight him,"
wheezed Bertie.

The very thought of this threw me into
a panic. Hand to hand combat, with

that monster?

"Let's keep going," I urged.

We ran on. Now I really did wish we'd left a trail. Nothing looked the same on the way back.

"This one!" I cried, spotting a familiar turning.

"No, that one!" hissed Bertie.

The truth was, we were

lost. Totally lost, in an underground maze as huge as the city above. Meanwhile, those nightmare footsteps were still following. The footsteps of a merciless, child-eating ogre.

Suddenly, Bertie seized up and leant against the scummy, crumbling wall, panting.

"Can't ... go further," he gasped.

This time I knew he meant it.

We had to act fast.

I pulled the stick from beneath my belt. "Put out the lantern," I ordered.

"But ... it'll be *pitch black*," protested Bertie.

"We've got to surprise him!" I hissed.

Bertie didn't argue any further. Next

second, the light was out, and Bertie was preparing his own weapon.

"You wait here," I said. "I'll go back towards him a bit. I'll try to trip him, then you batter him. Understood?"

I groped along the wall in the darkness, feeling the foul slime under my fingernails. We were like animals now, fighting for survival. Filth and smells meant nothing.

The footsteps grew closer. A light flickered ahead.

What was I doing? It was *stupid* to split up! Hastily I retraced my footsteps ... when, suddenly ...

THUNK!

My head was practically split like a walnut!

"Bertie, it's me!"

THUNK! THUNK! THUNK!

Bertie was going mental! Desperately I
tried to defend myself, trading blow for
blow, until both our clubs clattered onto
the sewer floor and Bertie finally came to
his senses.

"You stupid idiot!" he cried.

"*You* stupid idiot!" I yelled back.

"*Run!*" I cried.

Without a
lamp, without
weapons, and
almost without
hope, we
scrambled
off down the
tunnel. By
now the
King of the

Toshers was so close, his lantern gave a flickering light to us. Up ahead there was a turning. Maybe if we could get round there, and hide …

We made the turning. But at this point, our footsteps came to a dead halt. Ahead of us, to our total horror, the sewer was covered in a squirming carpet of fat, hideous rats.

"We're trapped!" cried Bertie.

By some incredible instinct, I looked up. High above us, by some miracle, was a drain cover.

"How can we get up there?" I croaked.

We looked desperately around.
No rope.
No rungs.
No ladder.

"Give me a lift!" said Bertie. "I'll get on your shoulders!"

I knitted my hands together to make a step. Bertie got his foot on it, then used me like a climbing frame. Once up on my

shoulders, he could reach the drain cover, which he shoved with all his might.

"Hang on a moment!" I said. "How am *I* going to get up?"

Crash! The cover was off. Bertie hauled himself up, off my shoulders, out through the escape hatch.

"Bertie!" I cried. "What about me?"

In disbelief, I heard Bertie's footsteps disappearing down the street.

I was as good as dead.

Frozen, like a rabbit faced by a fox, I watched the King of the Toshers making his way towards me, almost filling the cramped tunnel. With his bent head, his billowing coat and his sinister lantern, he could have been the Devil himself.

"Please," I pleaded, "I wasn't doing anything!"

But there was no mercy from the King of the Toshers. He stood above me, so close I could smell his stink, even over the stench of the sewer. Suddenly he raised a

gnarled hand, with one finger pointing.
The pointing finger came slowly, slowly
down, till it pressed right into my
quaking chest.

"Stanley!" he croaked. "I *told* you not
to come down
the sewer!"

7
Home

Dad made out that he was angry because I'd put myself in danger. But the real reason he was angry was that I'd found out his secret. He'd never been a shipping clerk, or a sewer inspector, or anything else for that matter. Every penny he ever

owned came from the sewers.

At least I knew why he smelled so bad.

I promised Dad I wouldn't tell a soul, and I kept my word. I never blamed him for what he did, because he was only trying to support his family. Everyone's got to survive somehow, just like those rats running round in the sewers.

We never raised the subject again. That

was a shame really, because I had so may questions I wanted to ask. Where did he get that coat with the big pockets? Did stooping make his neck ache? Most important of all, did he really eat those other toshers?

The London Sewers

Sewer beginnings

The first sewers were simply covered streams. Their main purpose was to carry away rainwater. But as towns expanded in the early 1800s, a better way of getting rid of both water and waste was needed.

The 1828 Police Act gave the police leaders the job of building new sewers. After this there was a huge increase in the building of sewers: these were far deeper and longer than the earlier ones. They were mainly built of bricks, usually in a U-shaped or an egg-shaped arch. However, most were still too small for a person to walk inside, and therefore could not be inspected properly.

London overflows

By the 1850s, all large cities had serious hygiene problems. Working-class areas were severely overcrowded, and waste from toilets (or "privies") caused severe pollution. Much of the filth found its way into the nearest river, which was usually where

drinking water came from. Flushing toilets (or "water closets") actually made river pollution worse. Disease was everywhere and the stench was unbearable. In 1858, London suffered a "Great Stink", in which the windows of Parliament had to be covered in sheets soaked in lime to keep out the foul smells.

Joseph Bazalgette

Something had to be done in London. A kind of town council was set up, called the Metropolitan Board of Works. A man called Joseph Bazalgette was given the job of designing new sewers.

Bazalgette's sewers were built between 1859 and 1865. They were far larger than anything which had gone before: up to 11 foot (3.35 metres) high. Their job was to intercept the old sewers and carry the waste away to pumping stations. From there, they were pumped away to sewage treatment works. As the old sewers no longer emptied into the Thames, the river became much cleaner. At least 318 million bricks were used in building Bazalgette's sewers, which are still in use today.

Other towns and cities also improved their sewer systems in the late 1800s. The treatment of sewage also improved. This was because people now understood that diseases were caused by germs, which travelled in waste water.

Sparks: Historical Adventures

ANCIENT GREECE
The Great Horse of Troy – The Trojan War
0 7496 3369 7 (hbk)   0 7496 3538 X (pbk)
The Winner's Wreath – Ancient Greek Olympics
0 7496 3368 9 (hbk)   0 7496 3555 X (pbk)

INVADERS AND SETTLERS
Boudicca Strikes Back – The Romans in Britain
0 7496 3366 2 (hbk)   0 7496 3546 0 (pbk)
Viking Raiders – A Norse Attack
0 7496 3089 2 (hbk)   0 7496 3457 X (pbk)
Erik's New Home – A Viking Town
0 7496 3367 0 (hbk)   0 7496 3552 5 (pbk)
TALES OF THE ROWDY ROMANS
The Great Necklace Hunt
0 7496 2221 0 (hbk)   0 7496 2628 3 (pbk)
The Lost Legionary
0 7496 2222 9 (hbk)   0 7496 2629 1 (pbk)
The Guard Dog Geese
0 7496 2331 4 (hbk)   0 7496 2630 5 (pbk)
A Runaway Donkey
0 7496 2332 2 (hbk)   0 7496 2631 3 (pbk)

TUDORS AND STUARTS
Captain Drake's Orders – The Armada
0 7496 2556 2 (hbk)   0 7496 3121 X (pbk)
London's Burning – The Great Fire of London
0 7496 2557 0 (hbk)   0 7496 3122 8 (pbk)
Mystery at the Globe – Shakespeare's Theatre
0 7496 3096 5 (hbk)   0 7496 3449 9 (pbk)
Plague! – A Tudor Epidemic
0 7496 3365 4 (hbk)   0 7496 3556 8 (pbk)
Stranger in the Glen – Rob Roy
0 7496 2586 4 (hbk)   0 7496 3123 6 (pbk)
A Dream of Danger – The Massacre of Glencoe
0 7496 2587 2 (hbk)   0 7496 3124 4 (pbk)
A Queen's Promise – Mary Queen of Scots
0 7496 2589 9 (hbk)   0 7496 3125 2 (pbk)
Over the Sea to Skye – Bonnie Prince Charlie
0 7496 2588 0 (hbk)   0 7496 3126 0 (pbk)
TALES OF A TUDOR TEARAWAY
A Pig Called Henry
0 7496 2204 4 (hbk)   0 7496 2625 9 (pbk)
A Horse Called Deathblow
0 7496 2205 9 (hbk)   0 7496 2624 0 (pbk)
Dancing for Captain Drake
0 7496 2234 2 (hbk)   0 7496 2626 7 (pbk)
Birthdays are a Serious Business
0 7496 2235 0 (hbk)   0 7496 2627 5 (pbk)

VICTORIAN ERA
The Runaway Slave – The British Slave Trade
0 7496 3093 0 (hbk)   0 7496 3456 1 (pbk)
The Sewer Sleuth – Victorian Cholera
0 7496 2590 2 (hbk)   0 7496 3128 7 (pbk)
Convict! – Criminals Sent to Australia
0 7496 2591 0 (hbk)   0 7496 3129 5 (pbk)
An Indian Adventure – Victorian India
0 7496 3090 6 (hbk)   0 7496 3451 0 (pbk)
Farewell to Ireland – Emigration to America
0 7496 3094 9 (hbk)   0 7496 3448 0 (pbk)

The Great Hunger – Famine in Ireland
0 7496 3095 7 (hbk)   0 7496 3447 2 (pbk)
Fire Down the Pit – A Welsh Mining Disaster
0 7496 3091 4 (hbk)   0 7496 3450 2 (pbk)
Tunnel Rescue – The Great Western Railway
0 7496 3353 0 (hbk)   0 7496 3537 1 (pbk)
Kidnap on the Canal – Victorian Waterways
0 7496 3352 2 (hbk)   0 7496 3540 1 (pbk)
Dr. Barnardo's Boys – Victorian Charity
0 7496 3358 1 (hbk)   0 7496 3541 X (pbk)
The Iron Ship – Brunel's Great Britain
0 7496 3355 7 (hbk)   0 7496 3543 6 (pbk)
Bodies for Sale – Victorian Tomb-Robbers
0 7496 3364 6 (hbk)   0 7496 3539 8 (pbk)
Penny Post Boy – The Victorian Postal Service
0 7496 3362 X (hbk)   0 7496 3544 4 (pbk)
The Canal Diggers – The Manchester Ship Canal
0 7496 3356 5 (hbk)   0 7496 3545 2 (pbk)
The Tay Bridge Tragedy – A Victorian Disaster
0 7496 3354 9 (hbk)   0 7496 3547 9 (pbk)
Stop, Thief! – The Victorian Police
0 7496 3359 X (hbk)   0 7496 3548 7 (pbk)
A School – for Girls! – Victorian Schools
0 7496 3360 3 (hbk)   0 7496 3549 5 (pbk)
Chimney Charlie – Victorian Chimney Sweeps
0 7496 3351 4 (hbk)   0 7496 3551 7 (pbk)
Down the Drain – Victorian Sewers
0 7496 3357 3 (hbk)   0 7496 3550 9 (pbk)
The Ideal Home – A Victorian New Town
0 7496 3361 1 (hbk)   0 7496 3553 3 (pbk)
Stage Struck – Victorian Music Hall
0 7496 3363 8 (hbk)   0 7496 3554 1 (pbk)
TRAVELS OF A YOUNG VICTORIAN
The Golden Key
0 7496 2360 8 (hbk)   0 7496 2632 1 (pbk)
Poppy's Big Push
0 7496 2361 6 (hbk)   0 7496 2633 X (pbk)
Poppy's Secret
0 7496 2374 8 (hbk)   0 7496 2634 8 (pbk)
The Lost Treasure
0 7496 2375 6 (hbk)   0 7496 2635 6 (pbk)

20th-CENTURY HISTORY
Fight for the Vote – The Suffragettes
0 7496 3092 2 (hbk)   0 7496 3452 9 (pbk)
The Road to London – The Jarrow March
0 7496 2609 7 (hbk)   0 7496 3132 5 (pbk)
The Sandbag Secret – The Blitz
0 7496 2608 9 (hbk)   0 7496 3133 3 (pbk)
Sid's War – Evacuation
0 7496 3209 7 (hbk)   0 7496 3445 6 (pbk)
D-Day! – Wartime Adventure
0 7496 3208 9 (hbk)   0 7496 3446 4 (pbk)
The Prisoner – A Prisoner of War
0 7496 3212 7 (hbk)   0 7496 3455 3 (pbk)
Escape from Germany – Wartime Refugees
0 7496 3211 9 (hbk)   0 7496 3454 5 (pbk)
Flying Bombs – Wartime Bomb Disposal
0 7496 3210 0 (hbk)   0 7496 3453 7 (pbk)
12,000 Miles From Home – Sent to Australia
0 7496 3370 0 (hbk)   0 7496 3542 8 (pbk)